ME
AND THE
MAN
ON THE
MOON·EYED
HORSE

ME
AND THE
MAN
ON THE
MOON·EYED
HORSE

by Sid Fleischman

Illustrated by Eric von Schmidt

An Atlantic Monthly Press Book
Little, Brown and Company
BOSTON   TORONTO

Books by Sid Fleischman

MR. MYSTERIOUS & COMPANY

BY THE GREAT HORN SPOON!

THE GHOST IN THE NOONDAY SUN

CHANCY AND THE GRAND RASCAL

LONGBEARD THE WIZARD

JINGO DJANGO

THE WOODEN CAT MAN

THE GHOST ON SATURDAY NIGHT

MR. MYSTERIOUS'S SECRETS OF MAG

MCBROOM TELLS A LIE

ME AND THE MAN ON THE MOON-EYED HORSE

TEXT COPYRIGHT © 1977 BY ALBERT S. FLEISCHMAN

ILLUSTRATION COPYRIGHT © 1977 BY ERIC VON SCHMIDT

FIRST EDITION

T 03/77

Library of Congress Cataloging in Publication Data

Fleischman, Albert Sidney.
  Me and the man on the moon-eyed horse.

  "An Atlantic Monthly Press book."
  SUMMARY: Young Clint's ingenious scheme foils a villainous train wrecker's attempt to rob the circus train.
  [1. Western stories. 2. Robbers and outlaws–Fiction. 3. Railroads–Trains–Fiction] I. Von Schmidt, Eric. II. Title.
PZ7.F5992Me   [Fic]   76-26595
ISBN 0-316-28571-4

ATLANTIC–LITTLE, BROWN BOOKS
ARE PUBLISHED BY
LITTLE, BROWN AND COMPANY
IN ASSOCIATION WITH
THE ATLANTIC MONTHLY PRESS

Published simultaneously in Canada
by Little, Brown & Company (Canada) Limited

PRINTED IN THE UNITED STATES OF AMERICA

Contents

In memory of Buddy Ryan

1

Sounds in the Night

I stood in my bare feet and peered out the window. Daybust was still a long way off. The desert wind had been singing like a tin whistle all night long.

Yes sir, it was going to be a mighty fine windy day, I thought. Maybe I'd race tumbleweeds with Gramps.

I went downstairs to kindle a fire in the big black kitchen stove. Then I went out back to fill the coffeepot with water from the pump.

The desert looked ghostly dark in the fading starlight. Our house was smack at the edge of town. Elvira said you could look farther and see less than from any spot on earth. She is my older sister.

I was back in the kitchen when I heard Elvira give a yell upstairs.

"Clint, you going to sleep all day?"

"Been awake for hours," I yelled back.

She appeared at the top of the stairs, brushing out her hair.

"Don't forget to kindle a fire," she said.

"Done it."

"*Did* it," she answered back. "And be sure to fill the coffeepot for Gramps."

"It's been did," I said.

"*Done.*"

"Elvira—make up your mind! Folks'll think you're bringing me up stupid."

I'd heard folks say it must be hard on Elvira having to mother me. She was only sixteen. Well, it was a lot harder on me. I couldn't get it through her head that I was old enough

4

to raise myself. I do believe she'd tell the devil how to kindle a fire.

I was fixing myself a pile of flapjacks when she came downstairs.

"Elvira," I said, "did you hear horses in the night?"

"What would horses be doing out in this wind?" she answered.

"Snortin' and whinnyin'."

"Imagination," she said. "Tumbleweeds skittering along, most likely." Then she slipped me a bright-eyed glance. "Circus train's coming through today."

I said, "Why didn't you tell me?"

"I just did."

I poured about half a jug of molasses on my flapjacks. Elvira had the day shift at the train depot, running the telegraph, and Gramps took it nights. By now I was certain she had spread the word to everyone in Furnace Flats. I reckoned I was the last to know.

"What time?"

"Twelve twenty-three."

Of course, the circus never stopped in a town as puny as Furnace Flats, Arizona.

Population 87—and sometimes I think that counted the cats and dogs.

But last year, as the train rattled on through, I'd almost got myself a good look at an elephant and a genuine camel.

A blast of wind lifted the red velvet curtains. "Drat this infernal climate!" my sister declared.

"Elvira—"

"I could shake an acre of grit out of those window curtains twice an hour."

She was almighty proud of those velvet curtains and everyone in town knew it.

"Elvira—"

"You get over to the depot and make sure Gramps isn't asleep on the job. Coffee'll be ready in a minute."

There were times when I couldn't slip a word in sideways. She could even talk with her fingers, tapping out Morse Code to Gramps when she didn't want me to know what she was saying. But now I knew my dots and dashes almost as well as she did.

I rapped my knuckles on the table. Gramps claimed code would raise a telegraph op' from the grave. "E-L-V-I-R-A."

She stopped her talking to ask, "What?"

"We could take the regular five-seventeen and follow the circus train," I said. "We'll buy us some tickets, front row, maybe. I've never seen a circus, Elvira, and neither have you."

The coffee was boiling hard and she dropped

in a couple of eggshells to settle the grounds. "Who'd run the telegraph? Woodpeckers, I suppose."

"I could go alone."

She handed me a pail with Gramps' breakfast packed in it. Then she lifted the coffee off the stove with a potholder.

"Better load your pockets with buckshot before you go out in the wind," she said, kind of smiling. "I wouldn't want a little fellow like you to blow away."

"Oh, hogwash," I answered.

She wanted to see a circus show as much as I did, I thought.

"Tell you what, Elvira. I'll go alone and tell you all about it."

She turned a long, soft look at me. I held my breath. Then she shook her head.

"Clint, you're too young."

2

The Message

I had to dodge tumbleweeds all the way to the train station. They skittered and bounced through town, and some flew by so fast you'd think they'd been shot out of a cannon.

There was a dim yellow light on in the depot even though it was already sunup. Gramps was asleep with his long legs propped on the desk and the green eyeshade pulled over his nose.

"Wake up, Gramps," I said, but I knew that he could sleep through thunder, lightning, and a ten-piece brass band.

So I reached over and jiggled the telegraph key. Quicker'n a gunshot his feet hit the floor, his swivel chair straightened, his eyes popped open, and his hand went for the pencil behind his ear. Then he saw me.

He clicked his store-bought teeth and said, "Howdy, Clint." He could clatterwack those teeth in Morse Code.

"It's daybust, Gramps."

He blew out the lamp. "And not a moment too soon. I'm dog-hungry."

"Elvira said the circus train's coming through today," I remarked.

"Ought to be mighty exciting."

I gave a shrug. "Reckon I'll skip it."

He was pouring himself a cup of hot coffee. He didn't say anything and it got kind of quiet in there. So I gave another shrug. "Circus special ain't worth shucks. It's nothing but another ol' train highballin' through."

"Expect you're right. I do miss the calliope music and the lions roaring. Saw a hippopotamus in Kansas City once. Mouth bigger'n a bathtub."

"I ain't never going to see a circus around here."

"Clint, I'd be surprised if there are three citizens of Furnace Flats who've even seen a circus parade, and the other two are liars."

"Elvira must think I'll fall off the edge of the earth if I get out of her sight."

"Your sister's right if you're thinking of chasing after that circus train. You'd worry her gray-headed. Me, too."

A tumbleweed flew past the window and Gramps clacked his teeth. "Look at that one!" he declared. "Doing sixty at least! Soon as my shift ends we'll pick out a couple of good ones and have a race."

"Figured on going fishing," I heard myself say. The idea came as a huge surprise to me.

"Might as well get going."

Gramps stood up from his breakfast. "By dabs, wish I could walk my legs a bit. Gettin' stiff-jointed." He glanced at the railroad clock on the wall. It was only a couple of minutes past six. "But I can't leave the telegraph. Two hours yet before I get off duty."

My ears pricked up. "Gramps, bet I could handle the telegraph key for you."

"Well, no. And I wouldn't want to keep a boy from fishing."

"Fish'll wait."

He rubbed his jaw and studied me hard. "Sure you wouldn't freeze up if the key starts chattering?"

"No, sir."

"I noticed you're getting mighty smart with your dots and dashes. I declare, maybe it's time to make a telegraph op' out of you."

I glowed up inside. He sat me down at his desk and slipped his pencil over my ear. Then he clacked his teeth in code. "U-R-I-N-C-H-A-R-G-E."

I was in charge! He went out into the wind and I had the whole depot to myself. The railroad was depending on me. I pulled the writing pad closer and held the pencil in my fingers, ready to take down any messages.

I fixed my eyes on the shiny brass telegraph key. It could come to life any second like the rattles on a snake.

I don't think I moved for ten minutes. I gripped the pencil tight. My fingers began to ache. But not a chirp came over the wire.

After a while I shoved the pencil back over my ear. I should have known there wouldn't be much telegraph traffic this hour of the

15

morning. Furnace Flats was such a no-account place it wouldn't surprise me if the railroad hardly remembered it had a no-account depot here.

I leaned back in the swivel chair and the pencil dropped off my ear to the floor.

Just then the telegraph key began to chatter away like forty crickets.

I dove to the floor for the pencil. My ears picked up the letters "FF FF FF." That was Furnace Flats.

That was me!

I pulled up the swivel chair and bent forward. My heart was thundering. Ever so gently I touched the brass key. It came to life. I tapped out "II" — the message that I was ready to receive.

Dots and dashes filled the air like a blast of buckshot. I wrote as fast as I could, barely keeping up. The message was to the sheriff of Furnace Flats from the sheriff of Greasewood, twenty-five miles east of us. Must be important, I thought!

I looked at the letters I had taken down.

S-T-E-P-A-N-D-A-H-A-L-F-J-A-C-K-S-O-N-G-A-N-G-H-E-R-E

S-E-N-D-P-O-S-S-E-E-V-E-R-Y-A-B-L-E-B-O-D-I-E-D-M-A-N

I must have got the first part wrong, I thought. Stepandahalf? Suddenly I realized that Gramps was looking over my shoulder.

"Jumping hop-toads!" he exclaimed.

"Reckon I got some of the letters mixed up."

"You run this over to the sheriff. You took it down exact."

"But what does it say?"

He ran a pencil mark between the words as he read it off.

"Step-and-a-half Jackson gang here. Send posse. Every able-bodied man."

"Who's Step-and-a-half Jackson?" I asked.

"A train wrecker. He robs the wreck. And always a step-and-a-half ahead of the law. First I heard he was in this part of the country!"

17

#

Dreadful Discovery

It was almost 7:30 when the sheriff and his men rode out of town. They seemed blown along with the tumbleweeds, but not near as fast.

Dust in the air turned the sun fox-colored. Before long you could hardly tell horses from tumbleweeds.

"I suppose you wish you were riding off with them," Elvira said.

I didn't answer.

"Unmerciful day to ride twenty-five miles," she went on.

"Powerful fine day," I declared. "And I aim to go fishing."

"Clint, I swear there are times when I think you're crock-headed. Fishing!"

"Mess of catfish in the creek."

"And soon as you pull 'em out the wind'll scale 'em for you, I suppose."

"Catfish don't have scales," I said.

"Oh, scat!" Elvira snapped. She was given to strong language like that.

She hurried back to the house now that the excitement was over and the men gone. If I knew Elvira she was going to beat the dust out of those brag curtains of hers before taking her shift at the depot. And that was even dumber than fishing.

But the general contrariness of it appealed to me. I got my willow pole and was digging up a can of worms behind the livery stable when Gramps gave me a shout.

I cut across the street to the depot.

"Clint," he said. "Do you know that Andy Carpenter over at Greasewood is the fastest brass-pounder on the line? And you got every word."

"Yes, sir."

"I'm almighty proud of you.—You know that. But I swear, many a time Andy's messages come over so lightning rapid I have to ask him to slow it down."

"Didn't seem much faster to me than you can clack your teeth, Gramps."

He shook his head, kind of puzzled. "Either you were born with telegraph wires for veins, or Light-fingered Andy sent the message with his great toe."

He returned to his desk. I set out along the railroad tracks toward the creek, heading straight into the wind. I tried to whistle, but it was kind of useless with the wind in my face.

But I felt like whistling. Not even Elvira would be able to take a message from Light-fingered Andy letter perfect. But I had. She'd have to pull in her horns a bit.

It was almost a mile to the creek. The cottonwood trees pitched and tossed as if they meant to pull up their roots from the creek bank.

I was almost there when I stopped short.

Dead ahead, a section of iron track was missing. Gone.

The Stranger

The rails had been pulled up, spikes and all, and tossed over the creek bank.

Step-and-a-half Jackson, I thought! Suddenly I remembered the sound of horses in the night. The train wrecker and his gang!

The circus special would come highballing through at midday and shoot clear off the rails.

I tossed down my willow rod and ran. Gramps could telegraph west to Opal Junction to hold the circus train.

With the wind behind me I skittered along as light as a roadrunner. But halfway to the depot I ran plumb out of breath. I stopped to get my wind.

Maybe it wasn't Step-and-a-half Jackson

who had lifted the rails, I thought suddenly.

Hadn't the message said he was in Grease-wood? That was a hard day's ride to the east of us. Step-and-a-half Jackson and his men couldn't have got here so fast.

I blue-streaked it the rest of the way. Maybe a crosscut wind had ripped out the rails. The wind could do tricksy things.

I hauled up at the depot. I had an ache in my side and I was panting like a hound looking for shade.

I noticed a moon-eyed horse tied up to the rail, and a string of three pack mules.

Elvira had come on duty, but Gramps was still there talking to a stranger. He was a huge, whisker-faced man in a dusty buffalo coat. A prospector, I thought.

He spit tobacco juice on the floor and Elvira gave him a look that would sour a pail of milk. "Don't this town have a sheriff?" he said. "Can't hardly find any menfolk to play a game of checkers."

"Gramps—"

"Formed a posse," Gramps said.

"You don't tell me."

"Gramps—" I still hadn't got my wind back.

That shaggy desert rat was fixing to spit again and Elvira shoved the cuspidor closer with her foot. He missed by a mile. "A posse! Who they after?"

"Step-and-a-half Jackson."

"Heavens and earth! The famous train wrecker?"

Gramps gave him a sudden all-over look and seemed to catch his breath.

But I had my wind back and blurted out, "Gramps! A section of track is missing!"

He cut me off, clatterwacking his teeth in code. "U GET OUT FAST."

"But Gramps, send a message down the line! They've got to hold the train at Opal Junction!"

Back came the rattle of his store-bought teeth. "THIS MAN MAY B STEP HALF JACKSON."

The stranger gave out an ugly roar of laughter. Quicker'n you could count to two he was waving pistols at us. "No maybes about it. That's me, in person. Hold still, or I'll blast you full of holes."

He could read code! He had understood every click and clack of Gramp's teeth.

"Now, sonny," Step-and-a-half Jackson said, "ain't nobody going to send word to Opal Junction or anywheres else. My men have cut the telegraph wires. In both directions."

5

"Iron Tooth Is Out There"

He picked up one of Gramp's red signal flags and waved it out a window. He crossed the floor and waved it out another window. Then he stopped and gave an angry shout. "Iron Tooth! Blast your ugly hide, I told you to keep the boys out of sight! Make yourselves scarce!"

No doubt about it, the gang had Furnace Flats surrounded.

He banged the window shut, muttering mostly to himself. "That long-nosed varmint don't have the brains of a flea." He used the butt of a gun to shatter Gramp's signal lanterns. Then he broke the signal flags over

27

a knee and set fire to them in the stove.

"Anyone dumb enough to try flagging down the next train will get a free buryin'," he said, kind of flush-faced and wild-eyed. Then he straightened his shoulders and chuckled a little. "But I can see you folks ain't that dumb. How'd you come to recognize me, ol' Gramps? I'm mighty flattered."

Gramps fixed him with a cold stare. "You're not as all-fired famous as you think. Not out here on the desert. You knew right off that Step-and-a-half Jackson was a train wrecker. You might as well have handed me your business card."

Elvira stood up. "I'm going home."

"No you ain't," said the outlaw. "I don't mind a bit of refined company to pass the hours. We'll just sit here until it's time for the wreck. Ol' Gramps, you play checkers?"

"Sir," I muttered, "reckon you don't know it's the *circus* special comin'." Despite myself, my eyes welled up. "Elephants and camels and trained horses. They'll be killed."

His eyebrows lifted. "A circus train? Even better! Bound to have a mighty full cashbox."

"It's a downright *cowardly* way to rob a train," Elvira snapped.

"Yes, ma'am," he grinned. "I shoot women and children, too."

I wiped my nose. You'd think Elvira would have sense enough to keep her mouth shut. "Mr. Jackson, you're meaner'n a barrel of rattlesnakes."

"I come by it naturally," he answered. "Runs in the family. There's so many of us Jacksons in hell, ma'am, our feet are sticking out the windows."

Through watery eyes I glanced at the clock ticking away on the wall. It was 8:36.

I tried to wipe my nose again without Step-and-a-half noticing. But he did. His eyes shifted angrily to me. "Sonny, who told you to hang around here and watch the clock for me?"

"I thought you said—"

"I don't want a leaky-nosed brat to start

29

bawlin' underfoot. You ain't needed. Go home and hide under the bed."

"I'm not bawling."

"Do what he says," Gramps scowled.

"And don't try to stir up any mischief," Step-and-a-half Jackson warned. "If the boys see you talking to anyone, I can't answer for what they'll do. Understand? Just remember that Iron Tooth is out there and he's mighty frolicsome with a six-shooter. Now get."

I walked as calm as I could, keeping my nose straight ahead, but trying to watch from the corners of my eyes. There was no one in the street, nothing but blowing tumbleweeds. The outlaws were keeping themselves well hid.

But I could feel dozens of cold eyes on me from rooftops and I didn't know where. The shut doors of the livery stable rattled in the wind. Were some of the men watching me through the cracks?

It wasn't fifty yards to the edge of town

and home. It seemed like fifty miles, and my heart was pumping away as if I'd run every step of it.

When I opened the door a stiff draft whipped up Elvira's red velvet curtains. I was right: she had beat every speck of dust out of them.

An idea came over me so quick that I could hardly remember to shut the door. By dabs! There might be a way to get a message to the posse and right under the noses of Step-and-a-half Jackson and his gang.

Tumbleweeds

I opened the side windows. I dashed from one to the other each time a tumbleweed bounced against the house. I snatched them inside. Iron Tooth and the others must have thought I was addled. Tumbleweeds weren't good for anything. Nobody fired a shot.

Before long the parlor was a jumble of tumbleweeds.

I pulled down one of Elvira's precious curtains. She'd skin me alive, but I ripped it into strips. They were red, weren't they? And everyone living along the railroad knew that red was a stop signal. Danger.

I set about tying a streamer to each tumbleweed. Tight to the stem. I ripped up curtain after curtain. Elvira would jump like a scalded cat when she walked in and saw her windows bare.

I checked again for outlaws. Then I opened a window on the other side of the house. Quick as I could I shoved and kicked tumbleweeds out the window.

They took off in the wind like great balloons. A whole regiment of them, leaping away with flapping red tails.

They highballed it east across the desert, straight for Greasewood.

If the wind didn't shift they ought to chase the posse quicker'n cannonballs. I reckoned most would go astray, but *some* were bound to catch up.

I shut the window and watched 'em bounce out of sight. But what if the posse thought we were just racing tumbleweeds? No, I thought, not with the same color rags — they'd be bound to notice that.

Yes sir, I told myself, they'd calculate something was wrong here in Furnace Flats. And if they snatched up one of those tumbleweeds and saw Elvira's brag curtains ripped up, they'd *know* something was wrong.

I opened the front door a crack and peered out. I wondered what Iron Tooth and the others were thinking. Well, none of them could out-gallop those red-tailed tumbleweeds now.

I shut the door and looked at the clock in the corner. It was 9:21. Three hours and two minutes before the circus train was due.

7

A Whistle in the Wind

I thought I'd jump out of my skin waiting.

I climbed up and down through the house looking out of one window and another.

Furnace Flats stood empty as a ghost town. There was nothing to hear but the rise and fall of the wind.

I didn't understand how Step-and-a-half Jackson's gang was keeping itself so well hid. I wondered if the train wrecker had signaled them to slip out of town, and I'd been too busy to notice. Yes, it wouldn't surprise me if they were already in the cottonwoods along the creek. Waiting like a flock of vultures for the train to run off the tracks.

I wasn't about to hide under the bed or bust into tears, either. Step-and-a-half Jackson calculated I wasn't grown up enough to have any sense. Just like Elvira. Well, he'd be monstrous sorry. And wouldn't she be surprised when the posse came trooping back!

But I wasn't patting myself on the back for taking down Light-fingered Andy's telegraph message letter perfect. For certain it was that infernal train wrecker himself who'd tapped into the line before cutting the wires. He wasn't any faster with his dots and dashes than a woodpecker with a sore beak.

But he'd got the menfolk out of town cleverly enough.

I about strained my eyesight watching for them. The desert seemed to stretch out forever, only farther, under the haze of dust.

Not even a jackrabbit was coming our way.

The posse would have to buck the wind every step of the way back. It might take hours, I thought.

If they were coming at all.

I went downstairs. The parlor clock was ticking away calm as you please. Dumb contraption, it would stand there shucking off seconds come death and destruction!

The minutes passed. The hours passed.

The clock struck noon.

Maybe the train would be late, I thought. But most likely it wouldn't.

Suddenly my skin went cold as a frog's. I thought I heard a train whistle carried along on the wind. It sounded like a faraway hound baying at the moon.

The Man on the
Moon-Eyed Horse

I lit out of the house.

The train was going to run off the tracks in about eighteen minutes—and doing a good forty miles an hour.

We could do *something*, couldn't we? Step-and-a-half Jackson must have left the depot by now, I thought.

But the moon-eyed horse was still tied to the rail with the string of pack mules.

My heart sank.

Then it bobbed right back up. I wanted a mule, but not Step-and-a-half Jackson to chase me without a good head start.

I looked around and then ducked under the horse's belly. I loosened the cinch. When I

finished I was amazed not to be shot full of holes.

He hadn't seen me.

I'd sneak up the line somehow. If Iron Tooth and the others noticed me they might not give a thought to a boy on a mule. I untied one of the animals, but before I could jump on there came Step-and-a-half Jackson out the door.

"Ma'am," he was saying to Elvira, "I shore pity the man that marries you. He'll be so henpecked he'll moult every autumn."

That was the bottom truth, and Elvira knew it. She turned beet red.

Then he saw me and shifted the big chaw of tobacco to his other cheek. "I thought I sent you to hide under the bed."

"I've never seen a train wreck before," I said, trying to keep my voice steady. "Maybe you'll let me ride along on one of your mules."

"You maybeed wrong. Them mules are for packing off the loot."

The train whistle came blowing along with

the wind again. It was still faint as a whisper.

"Looks like that train's going to be right on time," Step-and-a-half Jackson said.

He stuck his left boot in the stirrup, grabbed the saddle horn, and swung his other leg off the ground.

The saddle slipped quicker'n greased lightning. Step-and-a-half Jackson hit the ground like a roped steer.

If only he'd landed on his head!

He sat up in the dust. "I swallowed my last chaw of tobacco!" he bellowed. He grabbed out one of his guns and pointed it at me. "You flea-size, unscrupulocious little end of nothing! You messed with my horse!"

I looked into the barrel of his six-shooter, my heart a-thundering. "No sir," I muttered. "Just the saddle."

"I aim to crop your ears with hot lead."

Gramps yanked me off my feet by the collar and heaved me aside. And I do believe Elvira was going to tear into the outlaw like a wildcat. It surprised me.

"Elvira!" Gramps barked. Then, "Jackson, clear out before you get your name changed. 'Yellow-streak Jackson, the Orphan-shooter,' that's what folks'll call you. You'll be welcome as a skunk even among outlaws."

But I was no longer looking at the train wrecker or his six-shooter. I let out a yell.

"Posse's coming!"

9

The Train

I made out five shapes. The men were hunched over their horses' necks against the wind and grit. Only five had come back!

But Step-and-a-half Jackson didn't stop to count.

He jumped on his slip-saddled horse and rode off kind of bareback in a tangle of leathers. I watched him cut out across the wind. His moon-eyed horse looked kicking mad about going anywhere. The saddle was sliding around underneath and confusing his gait.

Deputy Jim Cozby, who was the town blacksmith except when the sheriff needed him, rode up. Three red streamers were blowing about in his fist. "What in tarnation's the trouble?"

"My velvet curtains!" Elvira squawked.

"Yes'm," the deputy said. "The sheriff reckoned it must be the end of the world, or worse, before you'd rip 'em up. He picked us out to ride back."

"And not a cussed second too soon," Gramps said.

"Step-and-a-half Jackson tore out a section of track," I said. "I saw it!"

"He can't be in Furnace Flats!"

"He is, and that was him you just saw riding out kind of sidesaddle," Elvira declared.

"Let's go, men," said Jim Cozby.

"No time to chase him!" Gramps snapped. "Circus special's due in twelve minutes and there's going to be a wreck. Engineer might misjudge us for train robbers flagging him down with our coats. There just might be time to reset the rails."

"I'll show you the exact spot!" I said.

Gramps fetched a sledgehammer. He climbed on a tall pack mule and so did I.

The men spurred their tired horses against the full blast of the wind. But those mules were fresh and perky, and Gramps and I found ourselves out in front.

Suddenly I remembered Iron Tooth and the rest of the gang. The creek bed must be

jumping with outlaws. As we approached a chill went up my neck.

Then came the wail of the train whistle.

We reached the gap in the rails. I looked around in the trees expecting to see a forest of rifles poke out at us.

I held my breath until the deputy and his men caught up. Not a flash of fire exploded from the trees. Where was that infernal gang hiding itself? Maybe they'd been scared off, I hoped.

I pointed and shouted. "The rails are down the bank! I'll look for spikes!" Then I added, "Could be outlaws about!"

The men carried their rifles and scurried down the bank.

I found one spike and then another. Still not a shot fired at us.

By dabs, I thought, there was no gang waiting for the train wreck!

Step-and-a-half Jackson would have headed straight for his men instead of cutting out alone across the desert. Yes sir, he'd made up that gang out of his head. I reckoned he'd made up Iron Tooth just to keep us jumpy.

He was a lone train robber, I calculated, that's why he wrecked 'em first.

It hardly seemed any time before the first

rail was in place. Gramps lifted the sledge and began hammering down the first spike.

"Here she comes!" someone yelled.

I peered into the wind. I could see the engine now, leading the circus special through the haze of dust like a trail of red ants.

"More spikes!" Gramps shouted at me.

The men hauled up the second rail quick as they could. But the engine was coming on even quicker, its headlamp blazing.

Jim Cozby took the sledge out of Gramps' hands and clanked away furiously at the spikes.

"Faster, men!" he yelled.

But we weren't going to make it, I thought. We weren't going to make it in time.

No sir. The train was coming down on us lickety-clack. There was going to be a terrible wreck and people killed, the clowns and the bareback riders, and the elephants and the camels, and what wasn't killed might have to be shot.

Gramps was already up the track, pulling off his coat as he ran.

But he didn't have a chance to wave it. Less than half a mile away the big engine wheels began to squeal and grind and scream along the tracks.

The engineer was trying to brake the train!

The great pistons slowed to a stop just a hoot and a holler up the line. All of us ran toward it. The engine sat breathing live steam and huffing black smoke.

"Great day in the mornin'," Gramps sighed, relieved but amazed.

The engineer stepped down from his cab. "Durned desert rats!" he snorted. "They know Arizona law better'n a pack of judges. I suppose you want a canteen of water too!"

I didn't know what he was talking about, but Gramps did. He clicked his teeth and smiled.

"Is that desert rat wearing a buffalo coat and riding a moon-eyed horse?"

"Yes and no. The horse was trying to kick

off its saddle. The man was crawling along
with the miseries. Holding his stomach and
dying of thirst. He's back up the tracks. And
the law says a train's *got* to stop on the desert
for any man in need of water.''

Gramps burst out laughing. "He's no desert rat. And it's not thirst he's dying of. It's the big chaw of tobacco he swallowed that's giving him the miseries."

"Boys," the deputy said. "Step-and-a-half Jackson must have looped around to throw us off his trail. Let's get him!"

The engineer's eyebrows jumped a mile. "The train wrecker?"

Gramps tossed his head in my direction. "It was Clint here discovered he'd ripped up a section of rails dead ahead. And if he hadn't loosened the rascal's saddle you wouldn't have stopped this train in time."

A tall man in a frock coat and a fancy green vest was striding toward us.

"What are we stopped for?" he asked.

The engineer nodded toward me. "It looks like this lad has saved your circus, Mr. Bigler."

10

Elephants on Main Street

Folks were standing in the wind to watch Bigler and Cooke's Colossal Circus and Congress of Wild Animals rattle through town.

But the circus train slowed, its steam whistle blowing. The engine pulled up at the depot and stopped.

"And you said people in Furnace Flats have never seen a circus parade?" Mr. Bigler asked me. I was sitting in a red plush chair in his private railroad car.

"Just Gramps," I answered. "And two folks fibbin' about it."

"Well, Clint, they're going to see one today."

Mr. Bigler led the parade himself! There was a brass band just behind him, and three genuine elephants, and a striped tiger hauled along in a golden cage, and clowns, and acrobats, and bareback riders standing on their horses, and a tooting calliope—and me.

55

When Elvira saw me she was surprised as a porcupine backing into a cactus. I was right there with Mr. Bigler, leading the parade.

It was a day folks weren't likely to forget. No sir, by dabs, not the day the circus stopped in Furnace Flats.

Even Step-and-a-half Jackson watched the doings. I saw him looking through the iron bars of the jailhouse.

The circus special had to clear the tracks for the regular afternoon train. We all stood watching and waving as the string of bright-painted cars clattered away.

Elvira hadn't said a word. I reckon she knew what she was going to find missing at home.

"Elvira," I said. "I'm plumb sorry about your brag curtains."

"Oh, good riddance," she answered. "They collected dust like flypaper. Clint, I *hated* those drat velvet curtains."

"You did?"

Her voice turned soft as goose down. "Clint, you could follow on the afternoon train and see the whole circus. Mr. Bigler is almighty indebted to you. You'd be his guest. I've been thinking you're getting old enough to tend to yourself."

I shot a surprised look at her. She was still standing on the depot platform with her eyes fixed on the circus cars disappearing down the track.

She'd give anything to see the whole colossal show herself. I could tell. And Mr. Bigler had said we'd be welcome forever, all of us.

"No," I said, finally. "That parade suited me just fine. I'm plumb tuckered out leadin' it, Elvira. Maybe the railroad'll fix it so we can all go next year, you and me and Gramps."

After a while she remarked, "You won't tell anyone what Step-and-a-half Jackson said about me."

"What did he say?"

"About me henpecking."

"Not unless I start moultin' come autumn," I said.

She looked at me and laughed.

R